JIM HEDGEHOG
and the Lonesome Tower

Russell Hoban

Illustrated by Betsy Lewin

CLARION BOOKS

New York

Clarion Books
a Houghton Mifflin Company imprint
215 Park Avenue South, New York, NY 10003
Text copyright © 1990 by Russell Hoban
Illustrations copyright © 1992 by Betsy Lewin
Text first published in Great Britain 1990 by Hamish Hamilton Ltd.

Printed in Singapore.

       Library of Congress Cataloging-in-Publication Data
Hoban, Russell.
  Jim Hedgehog and the Lonesome Tower / Russell Hoban ; illustrated by
Betsy Lewin.
     p. cm.
  Summary: Jim Hedgehog, who likes heavy metal music, buys a cassette
tape and a musical instrument from Mr. Strange, which lead him to a
haunted castle.
  [1. Heavy metal (Music)—Fiction. 2. Music—Fiction. 3. Hedgehogs
—Fiction.] I. Lewin, Betsy, ill. II. Title.
PZ7.H637Jij   1992
[E]—dc20   91-14340
                                               CIP
                                             AC

TWP 10 9 8 7 6 5 4 3 2 1

Contents

1
Strange Music

Jim Hedgehog liked his music loud and he liked it heavy. He listened to Giant Squid and Crashing Boars and Really Disgusting Things from the Deep Swamp. He listened to Truly Rotten and Monstrous Midnight and Gravedigger's Express. He listened to Antimatter and Beyond the Galaxy and Spacewind and Black Hole. He was always on the lookout for new heavy metal groups.

One Saturday Jim went with his mother to the market. All up and down the street were stands that sold fruit, vegetables, shirts, trousers, jackets, jumble, shoelaces, batteries, records, cassettes, umbrellas, and many other things.

While Mom was buying vegetables Jim went to the music stand. There was a stoat wearing dark glasses minding it. "Strange is my name and music's my game," he said. "If you don't see what you want, ask for it."

"Got any new heavy metal?" said Jim.

"Try this on your earholes," said Mr. Strange. He handed Jim a cassette with a handwritten label: Lonesome Tower.

"Is Lonesome Tower the album or the group?" said Jim.

"It's part of a building," said Mr. Strange.

"What's the group?" said Jim.

"It's a thing," said Mr. Strange.

"Why doesn't it say Itsa Thing on the cassette?" asked Jim.

"Cheap cassette," said Mr. Strange.

Jim listened to the beginning of the tape. It sounded like a hundred tomcats and a thousand bees in the middle of a hurricane. "That's not bad," he said.

"Hear any words?" asked Mr. Strange.

"Sure," said Jim. "Haven't you?"

"No, I haven't," said Mr. Strange. "What do you hear?"

Jim sang:

> "Crying in the sunshine,
> Crying in the rain,
> Trying for what went away
> And won't come back again."

"Was that last one crying or trying?" said Mr. Strange.

"Trying," said Jim.

"What do you think went away and won't come back again?" said Mr. Strange.

"I don't know," said Jim. "Do you?"

"No," said Mr. Strange, "I don't. If you like that cassette you can have it for a quarter."

"Why so cheap?" said Jim.

"I like to move things along," said Mr. Strange. He reached into the clutter at the back of the stand and took out a recorder. "Here's a nice little instrument," he said.

Just then Mom turned up. "Are you thinking of taking up the recorder?" she said to Jim.

"No," said Jim.

"You can have it for five dollars," said Mr. Strange to Mom, "and I'll throw in a book as well. He'll be playing tunes in a matter of hours."

"How many?" said Mom.

"Hours or tunes?" said Mr. Strange.

"Tunes," said Mom.

"One at least," said Mr. Strange.

Mom opened the book, *Strange Pieces for Beginners.* "There's only one piece in here," she said.

"I'll cross out the *s*," said Mr. Strange.

Mom paid Mr. Strange. "We can start this afternoon," she said to Jim.

"I have a lot of homework," said Jim.

"We'll find the time somehow," said Mom.

"Nobody ever got famous playing a recorder," said Jim.

"Nobody ever got deaf from it either," said Mom.

2
Green Bananas, Fat Alligators

When they got home Mom opened *Strange Pieces for Beginners.* "See," she said, "it's got diagrams and everything." She showed Jim how to go up and down the scale. "Now," she said, "we'll try this strange piece. It's called 'Lonesome Tower.' "

"That's the same title as my cassette," said Jim.

"Different music though," said Mom. "First let's sing it together. It's only got one verse." They sang:

"Something pacing on the tower
 Through the weary darkness long,
 Hour after lonely hour,
 Always seems to get it wrong."

"Odd song," said Jim.

"Yes," said Mom, "and it's odd that you were singing *after* me. Haven't they taught you to read music at school?"

"I must have been out sick that day," said Jim.

"I'll teach you now," said Mom.

"Harry Slime is lead guitarist for Giant Squid," said Jim, "and he can't read music."

"Maybe he's an orphan, but you've got me," said Mom. "From the bottom, the lines of the staff are E, G, B, D, F: 'Eating Green Bananas Doesn't Fatten.' "

"I'd have thought it would," said Jim.

"Those are just words to help you remember the letters," said Mom. "The spaces above the lines, reading up from the bottom, are F, A, C, E, G: 'Fat Alligators Cautiously Eat Grapefruit.' This song is in the minor key of . . ." She pointed to the G line. "What?"

"Grapefruit," said Jim.

"G is right," said Mom. "So where's do?"

"There isn't any dough in grapefruit," said Jim.

"Don't try to be clever," said Mom. "Do is the first note of the scale and it's on the G line where I'm pointing. How do we remember the lines?"

"Five Dozen Bellringers Gathering Eels," said Jim.

"You're doing it from the top down," said Mom.

"I'd rather start at the top than the bottom," said Jim.

"Do is on the G line," said Mom, "so the other notes go up the scale from there."

"Do, re, mi, fa, so, la, ti, do," said Jim.

"So fa, so good," said Mom.

3
To The
Haunted Castle

After the lesson Jim went for a walk beside a stream. He was thinking about "Lonesome Tower" and he was just about to play it when the recorder jumped out of his hands and threw itself into the water.

"I didn't think my playing was that bad," said Jim. As the recorder went downstream with the current he ran along the bank after it. He was hoping that it would come to a place where he could grab it without getting too wet. But the recorder kept to the middle of the stream, the stream ran deep and fast, and Jim ran with it mile after mile.

It seemed to Jim that he'd left home only a little while ago but already the sun was setting. The countryside around him had changed. He saw half-timbered cottages with thatched roofs and in the distance a castle high up on a mountain.

The evening mists were rising and an owl hooted. At a bend in the stream where the current was slow the recorder drifted in to the bank. Jim picked it up and shook the water out of it.

Nearby he saw the lights of an inn, The Haunted
Castle, and he heard voices and the clink of glasses.

When Jim opened the door the talking stopped
and everyone turned to look at him. The innkeeper
was a stoat wearing dark glasses.

"Mr. Strange!" said Jim. "What are you doing
here?"

"I live here," said Mr. Strange. "Learned that tune yet?"

"Yes," said Jim.

"Good," said Mr. Strange. He went outside and closed the wooden shutters on all the windows. Then he closed the door and barred it.

4
Itsa Thing Live

"Why did you do that?" said Jim.

"It gets noisy around here," said Mr. Strange.

"You mean frogs and crickets, that kind of thing?" said Jim.

"No," said Mr. Strange. "I mean . . . " Just then there came a noise like five thousand tomcats and ten thousand bees in the middle of two or three hurricanes. It shook the inn and rattled the windows and all the glasses on the bar. Mr. Strange covered his ears and crept under a table. So did everyone else but Jim.

"THAT'S ITSA THING LIVE," said Jim. He had to shout so that Mr. Strange could hear him. "THEY REALLY SOUND GOOD."

"IT ISN'T THEY, IT'S IT," said Mr. Strange. "IT'S THE THING THAT WALKS THE CASTLE TOWER."

"WHAT KIND OF A THING?" said Jim.

"NOBODY'S EVER GOT PAST THE NOISE TO FIND OUT," said Mr. Strange.

"I CAN HEAR WORDS," said Jim:

"HOLLERING AT MIDNIGHT,
HOLLERING AT NOON,
HOLLER ALL THE HOUSES DOWN
IF I DON'T FIND IT SOON.

WHAT'S IT TRYING TO FIND?"

"NOBODY KNOWS," said Mr. Strange. "TRY PLAYING YOUR RECORDER AND SEE IF ANYTHING HAPPENS."

Jim played "Lonesome Tower" and everything went quiet. "Maybe it wants help," he said. "I'm going up there."

"Be careful," said Mr. Strange.

"Maybe you'd like to come with me," said Jim.

"You're the one who hears the words," said
Mr. Strange. "You'll do better alone."

"Here I go then," said Jim, and off he went into
the night.

In the moonlight Jim could clearly see the castle standing dark and lonely on the mountain. In the silence he felt something holding its breath and waiting for him.

Jim found the path and started the climb to the

castle. His footsteps and his breathing sounded
very loud to him, and the stones loosened by his
feet seemed to crash and thunder as they went
rolling down the mountain behind him. He heard
the hooting of an owl and the squeaking of bats.

The moonlight through the windows made silvery shapes on the floor of the empty hall. Jim made his way to the door of the tower, then up the winding stairs. When he stopped to listen there was only silence.

When Jim was near the top of the stairs he thought he heard something sniffling. What if it's something huge and really dreadful? he thought. All I can do is roll up in a ball and make myself as spiky as possible.

Jim came out into the open at the top of the
tower. In the bright moonlight he saw something
by the parapet. It wasn't very big.

"Who are you?" said the thing.

"Jim Hedgehog," said Jim. "Who are you?"

"Itsa Thing," said the thing.

"*What* are you?" said Jim.

"I'm a girl thing," said Itsa.

"I mean what kind of thing," said Jim. "What
do you do?"

"I'm a tower-walking thing," said Itsa. "Lots of castles have them."

"I think your 'Lonesome Tower' is a terrific sound," said Jim.

"I don't know what you mean," said Itsa.

"Crying in the sunshine," said Jim, "crying in the rain, trying for what went away and won't come back again."

"Oh, that," said Itsa. "I must have sounded really awful making all that noise, but when I get upset I can't help it."

"Why were you upset?" said Jim.

"Walking towers is dead boring unless you have a little song to sing," said Itsa, "and it's got to be exactly right for the particular size and shape of the tower. I'd been working on a song for years and I finally had just the thing for this tower. Then it dropped right out of my mind and I haven't been able to remember it since. I keep trying but I never get it right."

"Why didn't you write it down?" said Jim.

"It didn't have any words," said Itsa.

"But didn't you write down the notes?" said Jim.

"What do you mean, 'write down the notes'?" said Itsa.

"I'll show you," said Jim. He found a pencil
stub and a scrap of paper in his pocket and he drew
a staff. "First you have to know where the green

bananas and the alligators go. Or it could just as well be Eighty Grunting Bears Doing Fireworks or Fish And Chips Eaten Greedily, if you see what I mean."

"Did you say grunting bears?" said Itsa.

"Yes," said Jim. "Why?"

"Bears like honey," said Itsa. "Honey's made by bees. Bees get nectar from flowers. My little song is coming back to me, I was thinking of bees and flowers when I made up the tune. It goes like this," and she hummed it.

Quickly Jim wrote down the notes of Itsa's song, then he showed her how to do it. "Now you'll never lose it again," he said.

"This time I'll put words to it," said Itsa. She sang:

"Sweet as nectar from the flowers,
  Music makes for happy hours—
  In my songs will always be
  Notes Jim Hedgehog brought to me."
"That's very nice," said Jim.
"You don't like it," said Itsa. "I can tell."
"I like it," said Jim. "I guess I'm just used to
your heavy metal sound."

"You mean like this?" said Itsa, and her voice came out like five thousand tomcats and ten thousand bees and two or three hurricanes:

**"SWEET AS NECTAR FROM THE
   FLOWERS,
   ROCK AND ROLL THE HAPPY
   HOURS—
   IN MY SONGS WILL ALWAYS BE
   NOTES JIM HEDGEHOG
   BROUGHT TO ME."**

"Wonderful," said Jim.

"But I won't sing like that all the time," said Itsa, "only for you."

"Maybe you can visit my school for the Summer Festival," said Jim.

Itsa did, and she was a big success. Windows shattered for miles around.